Walt Disney's
One Hundred and One Dalmatians

A GOLDEN BOOK • NEW YORK
Western Publishing Company, Inc., Racine, Wisconsin 53404

Not long ago in a London apartment a handsome Dalmatian dog named Pongo lived with his pet human. Pongo's pet was called Roger, and he was a musician of sorts. He sat at the piano, writing songs of love—something he knew nothing about. Pongo was bored with their bachelor life, and he thought it was time Roger got married.

Pongo knew that dogs were poor judges of human beauty, but he had a rough idea of what to look for. As he watched from his window a student came by with an Afghan hound. "The wrong type," Pongo said to himself.

Next came a fancy lady with a poodle. "Too fancy," said Pongo.

Pongo realized how difficult it would be to find the right type. Then suddenly he saw a young woman with a Dalmatian. He thought she—the Dalmatian—was the most beautiful creature on four legs. They were heading for the park.

"If only I can arrange a meeting," thought Pongo.

He jumped down from the window seat and made so much fuss that Roger stopped working to take him for a walk. In the park he dragged Roger toward the woman and wrapped his leash around their legs.

Before they knew it, Roger and the young woman fell into a pond—not their idea of fun!

But Pongo's trick worked. Roger and the young woman, whose name was Anita, fell in love and got married. Anita's dog, Perdita, and Pongo fell in love, too. They all moved into a small house near the park. It wasn't long before Perdy was expecting puppies.

One day Cruella De Vil, an old school friend of Anita's, came to visit. Nanny, the housekeeper, let Cruella in. Perdy took one look and ran into the kitchen to hide under the stove.

"Hello, Cruella," Anita said. "How are you?"

"Miserable, darling," said Cruella. "As usual, perfectly wretched.

"Now, the puppies," Cruella went on. "Where are they?"

"Perdy's puppies aren't due for at least three weeks," Anita said. "But, Cruella, isn't that a new fur coat?"

"My only true love, darling," Cruella crowed. "I live for furs. I worship them. Is there a woman in all this wretched world who doesn't? But I must rush. Let me know the moment the puppies arrive!" And she was gone.

Perdy's puppies arrived right on time.

"The puppies are here!" cried Nanny. "Fifteen of them. And the mother's doing fine."

Then she brought in a tiny puppy that seemed to be dead. But Roger rubbed it gently, and soon it started moving.

"Imagine, fifteen puppies!" Anita said in wonder.

"Fifteen puppies!" cried a voice from the doorway. It was Cruella. "I'll buy them all!" she shrieked, taking a check and shaking her pen.

Roger was covered in ink spots. "We're not selling the puppies," he said firmly. "Not a single one!" Anita was delighted.

"Why, you horrid man!" Cruella hissed. "Keep the little beasts, for all I care. But I'll get even with you!" And she stormed off.

"My pet, Roger, told off that devil woman," Pongo said to Perdy. "She's gone, and our puppies are safe." They lay down with their puppies, as happy as they could possibly be.

The puppies grew up quickly. They loved watching TV.

"Old Thunderbolt's the greatest dog in the whole world," said Lucky, his eyes glued to the screen.

"He's even better than Dad," said Patch.

"*No* dog's better than Dad!" said Penny.

"Come on, Thunderbolt!"
cried Patch. Lucky was
so excited that he put
his paws up by the screen.
"Down, Lucky, dear,"
said Perdy gently. "As
soon as this is over, it
will be time for bed."

That night Pongo and Perdy went for their usual walk with Roger and Anita, while Nanny put the puppies to bed. Just as she tucked them in, the doorbell rang.

Two shady-looking characters were standing on the doorstep.

"Good evening, ma'am," said one. "We're here to inspect the wiring and switches."

They pushed past Nanny, who followed But they locked her in an upstairs room.

When Nanny at last got free, she found that all the puppies were gone. Meanwhile, the two villains were on the phone to Cruella. They told her that the job was done.

"So you've got the little darlings," she sneered.

When the police found no trace of the puppies, Pongo decided to try the twilight bark, the dogs' gossip network. "If our puppies are anywhere in the city, the London dogs will know," said Pongo. "We'll send word tonight."

Pongo barked across the city and waited for a reply. He soon heard the deep bark of a Great Dane, who received the message that fifteen Dalmatian puppies had been stolen.

The Great Dane barked the message on to other dogs, until finally it was heard by Towser out in the country.

"I'd better give the news to the Colonel," Towser said to Lucy the duck. "He's the only one in barking range. I'll bark all night if I have to."

The Colonel was an old dog who lived in a nearby barn with his captain, a horse, and his sergeant, a cat called Tibs. He didn't get many messages on the twilight bark, and it took him a while to decode the news. "Puppies stolen," he said at last.

"That's funny," said Tibs. "Two nights ago I heard puppies barking over at Hell Hall."

"No one's lived there for years," said the Colonel. "But let's go."

Tibs crept up to the old house and slipped through an open window. To his amazement he saw a room full of Dalmatian puppies being guarded by two shady-looking characters.

Some puppies were watching TV. One older pup told Tibs, "That bunch has collars. They're not from the pet shop."

Tibs reported back to the Colonel. "There are ninety-nine puppies in all, and the stolen ones are among them."

The Colonel barked a report to Towser, who passed it on. At last the news reached London. When Pongo heard it, he and Perdy left home at once to find their puppies. Outside of London, they ran into a snowstorm. But even that couldn't stop them.

Tibs crept back to Hell Hall just as Cruella arrived. "The job must be done tonight," she told the two dognappers. "I'll settle for a half-dozen coats. I don't care how you kill the little beasts. Just do it!" Cruella screeched as she rushed out.

"So that's it—dog-skin coats!" thought Tibs. He knew he had to act fast. Now was his chance, while the men were watching TV.

Tibs told the pups
to sneak out of the
room through a
hole in the wall.
The villains were
laughing so hard
that they didn't
even notice the
pups creeping past.

Then the two men began discussing who would do the dirty work. "I'll pop them on the head," said one, "and you do the skinning."

"Hey, look!" said the other man. "They've gone. Here, grab a flashlight and let's go find them!"

Tibs heard the men coming, and he pushed the puppies under the stairs.

But Tibs knew it wouldn't be long before they were found. The villains chased the puppies all over the house until at last they had them cornered.

"We've got them," they said with glee.

But just at that moment there was a loud crash. Two dogs came flying through the window and stood before the villains, teeth bared. Pongo and Perdy were just in the nick of time.

Now it was the villains' turn to be chased around the house. Tibs quietly led the puppies outside, and soon Pongo and Perdy joined them. They left the villains to face Cruella.

Pongo and Perdy were delighted to see their puppies again and furious about the dog-skin coats. "We must get back to London," Pongo said. "We'll take all the puppies home with us." And so Perdy led them off through the snow.

After miles of walking, the puppies were very tired.

"My nose is froze, and my toes are froze," Lucky said to Pongo.

Fortunately a collie told them about shelter at a nearby dairy farm. The cows felt sorry for the puppies and let them rest there.

The next stop on the journey was the house of a friendly Labrador. The Dalmatians knew that Cruella and her men were on their trail.

But Lucky and Patch were still full of mischief. They played in the fireplace and were soon covered with soot. When Pongo saw them, an idea struck him. He, too, rolled in the soot.

"The Labrador said he could get us a ride home in a van," Pongo to Perdy. "To hide from that devil woman, we'll all be Labradors! Come on, kids, into the soot!"

The puppies didn't need to be told twice. They had always wanted to get really dirty. Then they crept out to the van.

But the snow
washed off some of
the soot. Just then,
Cruella's car came
past, and she saw a
spotted puppy.

"There they go!"
she shouted, roaring
after the van.

Cruella's car was right behind the van, and her two men took a different road in their truck. Suddenly Cruella drew right up alongside the van and tried to force it off the road. Sparks flew, but the van driver managed to stay on the road. Cruella dropped back.

Perdy and Pongo could see Cruella's mad face as they clung to the van. She was trying to ram it from behind, and her face terrified them.

The villains' truck, on the other road, looked as if it were going to collide with the van. But it smashed into Cruella's car instead.

"You idiots!" she shrieked, picking herself up.

When the Dalmatians
got home, Roger and
Anita were joyful.

"Pongo, boy, is that
you?" Roger asked,
wiping off the soot.

"Perdy, my darling,"
said Anita, "and the
puppies—a *lot* of
puppies!"

Roger started
to count them all.

"A hundred and one Dalmatians," said Roger.
"What will we do with them?" Anita asked.
"Keep them!" Roger replied. He played and sang,
"We'll have a plantation, a Dalmatian plantation."
Pongo and Perdy were as happy as could be.